ISBN: 978-0-7641-6898-7
Library of Congress Control Number: 2017930320
Date of Manufacture: March 2017
Manufactured by: Hung Hing Offset Printing
Company, Ltd, New Territories, Hong Kong
Printed in China   9 8 7 6 5 4 3 2 1

First edition for the United States and Canada
published in 2017 by Barron's Educational Series, Inc.

First published in 2017 by Scholastic Children's Books,
Euston House, 24 Eversholt Street, London NW1 1DB
A division of Scholastic Ltd.

Text copyright © 2017 Chae Strathie
Illustrations copyright © 2017 Nicola O'Byrne

All inquiries should be addressed to:
Barron's Educational Series
250 Wireless Boulevard, Hauppauge, NY 11788
www.barronseduc.com

With love to Alex and Louisa,
who are slightly smaller
than a T. Rex.
C.S.

For my favorite dinosaurs,
Strawberatops, Emmadactyl,
Pauliinasaurus, and Chaealodon.
N.O.

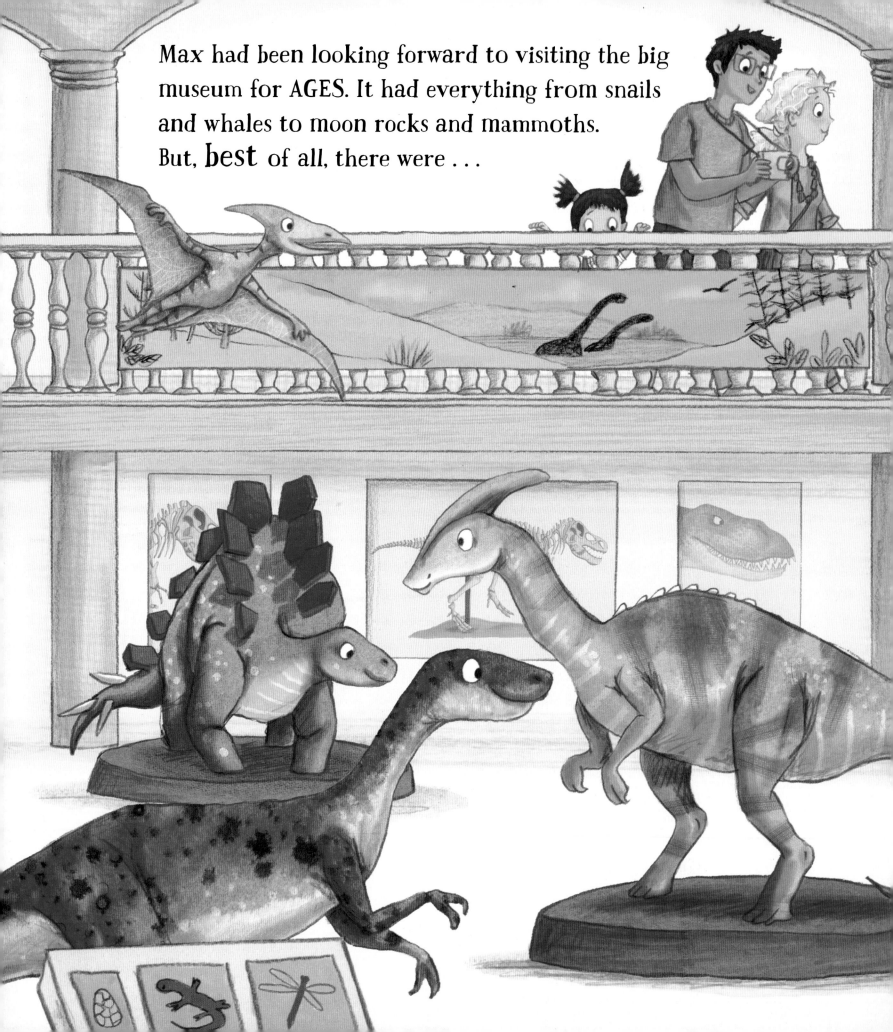

Max had been looking forward to visiting the big museum for AGES. It had everything from snails and whales to moon rocks and mammoths. But, best of all, there were . . .

...DINOSAURS!

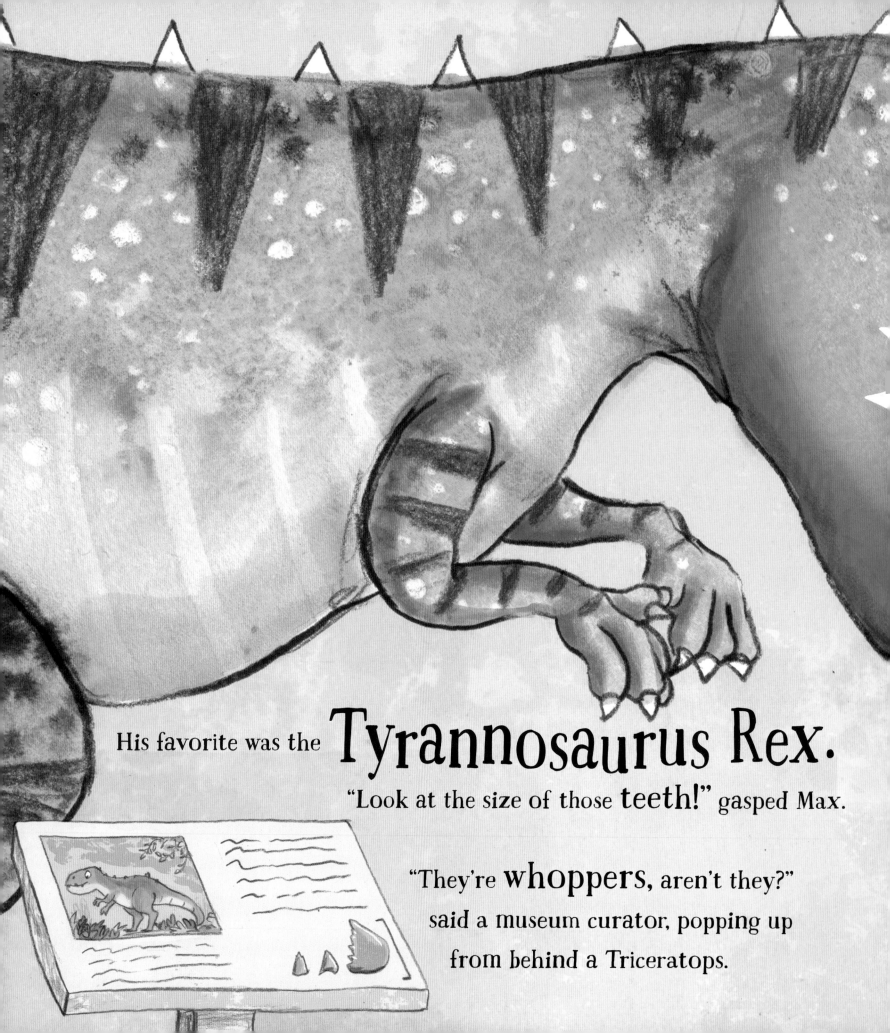

His favorite was the Tyrannosaurus Rex.

"Look at the size of those teeth!" gasped Max.

"They're whoppers, aren't they?"
said a museum curator, popping up
from behind a Triceratops.

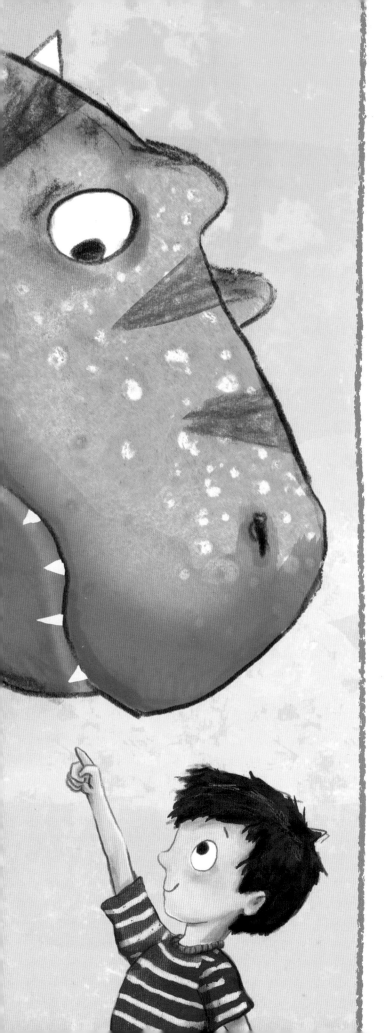

"They call me **Dinosaur Dora**," she said. "We're about to close, but you can come back any time."

"We live too far away," sighed Max. "And I have LOTS of questions."

"Well, why don't you write our T. Rex a **letter?**" said Dinosaur Dora. "He might even write back!"

When Max got home, he got to work.

Dear Dinosaur,
I came to see you today.
You are my favorite dinosaur
in the whole world. Would you
mind if I asked you some questions
about being a dinosaur?

Bye for now,

Max

Max

He put the letter
in the mailbox.

Then he waited.

 And waited.

 Until one morning...

Max the small human
105 Short Road
Village Far Away

There was a **reply!**

Carnivores by Emmadactyl Drage

How Many Teeth? by Chaeompsosaurus

How Big Was The T-Rex? by Paularaptops

Dino Facts by Stegostrawous Berrie

"Yikes!" said his mommy.

"I'm not scared," said Max.

"This one's for you, Rex!"

Dear Dinosaur,
That was quite rude. There's no need to show off. Here's how loud I can roar.

Rooooaaaarrrr!

It's not quite as impressive, but I'm only six and I don't have a head the size of a sofa like you do.

I was wondering what you eat? Have you ever had a sausage? I could send you one if you like. I have to go for my bath in a minute. What is your favorite bath toy?
Bye for now,

Max

P.S. Can you write, or does somebody have to help you?

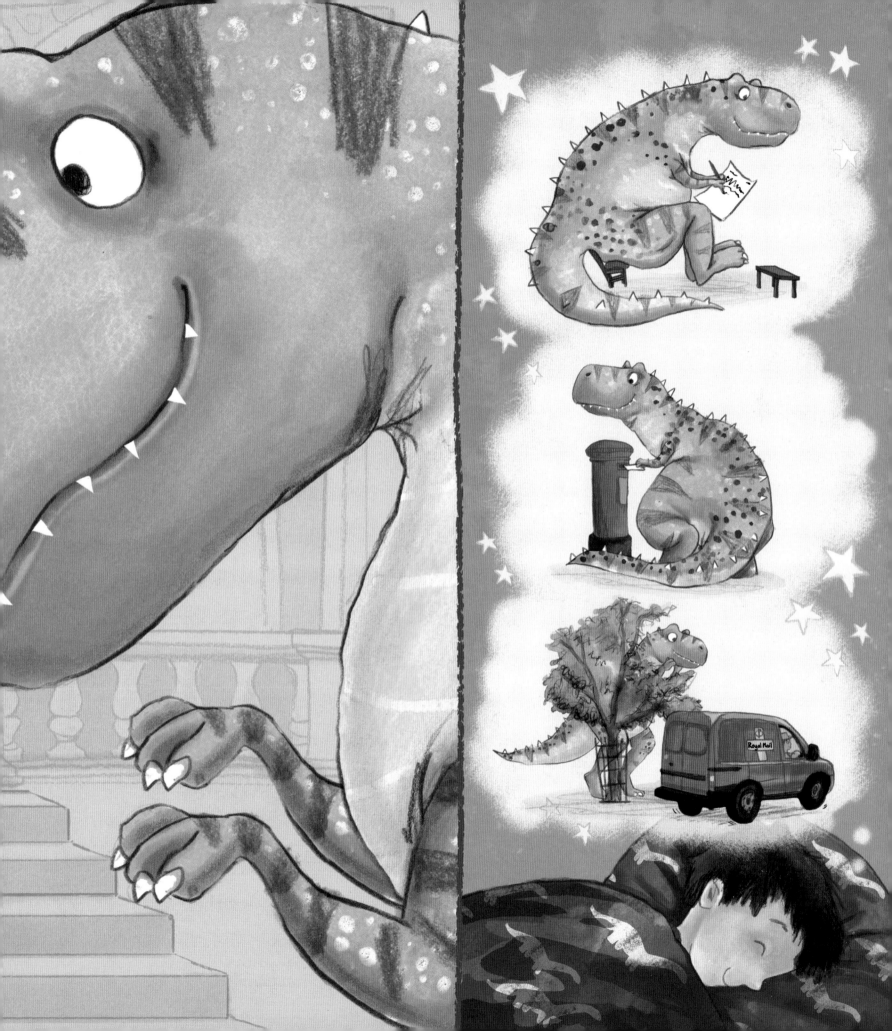

THE CITY MUSEUM

Natural History & Conservation

Dear Max,

Of course I can write! That's why T. Rexes have such small hands—so we can hold a pencil.

I have never had a sausage. I mainly used to eat other dinosaurs. My favorite was Triceratops. It's a bit embarrassing, as my best friend here at the museum is a Triceratops. We don't talk about food much.

Please do not send me a sausage. Unless it is a Sausagesaurus the size of a house.

I sometimes have a dip in the fish pond. I don't think the fish are too happy. I do not have a bath toy.

If you are six that means I'm 65,999,994 years older than you! Actually, it's my birthday next week.

ROOOOOAAAAAAAAR!!

Yours scarily, **T. Rex**

MIDDLE STREET SQUARE · GREENVILLE, SC · 29612

THE CITY MUSEUM
Natural History & Conservation

Dear Max,

You don't seem to be nearly as scared as you should be. Your legs should have turned to jelly by now.

Thank you for your card and rubber duck. I'm really looking forward to my next dip. We had a birthday party here after everyone went home. Then we played soccer, just like you. It was fun until the mammoth knocked over a 2,000-year-old vase with his bottom.

ROOAAARRR!!

Yours dinosaurly,

T.Rex

P.S. I can run **really** fast. I would probably win ALL the races at your school field day.

MIDDLE STREET SQUARE · GREENVILLE, SC · 29612

Dear Dinosaur,

I have some VERY exciting news.
Yesterday my very first tooth fell out! Dad
said a big one will grow in its place. I have
sent you the tooth, as I will not be needing it.
Bye for now,

Max

P.S. I went to see my sister, Millie,
in her ballet show yesterday.
She had to wear a pink tutu.
Imagine if dinosaurs did ballet!

THE CITY MUSEUM
Natural History & Conservation

Dear Max,

Thank you for the tooth. It is so TINY! MY teeth are a bit bigger than that. Some are as long as a ruler! And my bite is three times stronger than a lion's.

I have a pal here called Compsognathus. He is only a little bigger than a chicken— one of the smallest dinosaurs ever! He was missing a tooth . . . and yours looks splendid in the space.

Now YOU'RE part of a dinosaur! Perhaps we should call you MAXOSAURUS REX!

Yours toothily,

T.Rex

P.S. I would like to see a dinosaur ballet! I might get Triceratops to dress up in a pink tutu. Tee hee!

MIDDLE STREET SQUARE · GREENVILLE, SC · 29612

^ "Thanks, Rex!"

Greetings

max@seashellcottage.co.dino

Happy Holidays!

Dear Max,

I wish I were on vacation with you.

Imagine the sandcastle I could build!

Speaking of sand, the desert is the best place to find bones and fossils.

I look forward to seeing you soon, and promise not to eat you.

Your friend,

T.Rex

P.S. Of COURSE it is ME writing to you.

Silly grown-ups!

Back at the museum, Dinosaur Dora was fussing around the Triceratops when Max and his parents arrived.

"Something **funny** has been going on here," she said.

"The **Triceratops** is **wearing a tutu,**

there's definitely something **different** about that little one's **smile . . .**

. . . and

...the T. Rex just won't let go of that rubber duck."